Dear Parents and Teachers,

Reading chapter books is a very excii [...] child's life as a reader.

With Hello Reader Chapter Books, our goal is to bring the excitement of chapter books together with appropriate content and vocabulary so that children take pride in their success as readers.

Children like to read independently, but you can share this experience with them to make it even more rewarding. Here are some tips to try:

- Read the book aloud for the first time.
- Point out the chapter headings.
- Look at the illustrations. Can your child find words in the text that match the pictures?
- After you or your child finishes reading a chapter, ask what might happen in the next chapter.
- Praise your child throughout the reading of the book.
- And if your child wants to read alone, then take out your own book or magazine and read sitting side by side!

Remember, reading is a joy to share. So, have fun experiencing your child's new ability to read chapter books!

Francie Alexander
Vice President and Chief Academic Officer
Scholastic Education

To Erika, Mara, and Scott—the apples of my eye.
— E.S.H.

For my sister, Mrs. Berglund,
and her kindergarten class.
— A.V.K.

ISBN 0-439-57396-3

12 11 10 9 8 7 6 5 4 3 2 1   3 4 5 6 7 8/0

Printed in the U.S.A.
First printing, September 2003

We All Fall for Apples

By Emmi S. Herman
Illustrated by Anne Kennedy

SCHOLASTIC INC.
New York   Toronto   London   Auckland   Sydney
Mexico City   New Delhi   Hong Kong   Buenos Aires

Chapter 1

We are going to the farm.
We are going to pick apples.

Wait for Ruff!
Ruff wants to go, too.

We are going to the farm.
We are going to drink cider.

Wait for Sam!
Sam wants to go, too.

We are going to the farm.
We are going on a hayride.

Wait for Jan!
Jan wants to go, too.

We are going to the farm.

We are going to wait
for a new tire!

Chapter 2

We can fill a basket.
We can fill it with apples.

Oh, no! Too many apples.

We can fill a cup.
We can fill it with cider.

Oh, no! Too much cider.

We can fill a bag.
We can fill it with hay.

Oh, no! Too much hay.

We can fill a wagon.
We can fill it with people.

Oh, no! Too much fun!

We can fill a car.
We can fill it with sleepy people.

Too tired!

Chapter 3

Sam is making apple jam.

Mix and mash.
Add a dash.

Let it stand.

Jan is making apple bread.

Mix and mash.
Add a dash.

Let it bake.

Let it rise.

Apple jam and bread surprise!